Printed in China

This book was published by Pat
Arnold and printed by www.
margaretmouse.com.

ISBN 0-9761326-1-3

Note from Margaret...

Hi!
I am so glad you decided to get "The Picnic"!

I know you will have lots of fun reading about my adventures in and around the Barnyard. Here's a list of my upcoming adventures!!

"Pretty is as pretty does"

School Days–
Catch your breath with Margaret and Sally as they learn first-hand why safety rules are made.

Hide 'n Seek–

Learn what it means to play the game and not win.

Harvest Carnival–
Read about how it feels to be 'different' from others.

Snow Mouse–
See how someone with a handicap saves the day.

Have fun reading–and learning!
Margaret Mouse

Visit my website!
www.margaretmouse.com

This Book Belongs To

Given By

The Picnic

Adventures at Play

Story: Cherokee Wyatt
Illustrations: Angela M. Redmon

"Good Morning, good morning," sang Cherry Chickadee as Margaret Mouse and her friend, Maria Mouse, walked beneath her Cherry Tree home in the Orchard.

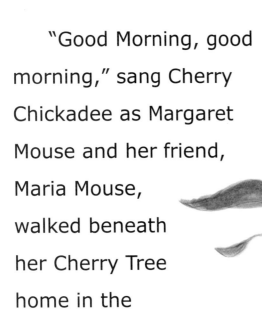

"Isn't my tree so beautiful all filled with bright red cherries?"

"Yes, very pretty," answered Maria. "We're going to a picnic by the Pond with the Duck family. Would you like to come along?"

"No, no. I'm going to stay home, because a spring storm is coming," answered Cherry. "A storm!?" Margaret scoffed. "Cherry, the sun is bright and there are no clouds in the sky."

"Maybe, but I still think there will be a storm today. You should be careful," warned Cherry as the girls turned to leave.

"We will," Maria answered as they walked away. Maria walked slowly because she used crutches due to losing a leg in a trap when she was younger.

In a short time, the two girls came upon Rembrandt, the Writing Spider. He was busily working as he caught sight of the girls. **"Hallo, mes amies!"** he shouted. Rembrandt was *always* shouting because of his hearing problem.

Margaret backed up a few steps as she answered, "Fine, Mr. Rembrandt. What are you working on?"

"Ah, my latest work --- eeet will be a masterpiece!" JUST AT THAT MOMENT, the web shook so badly that Rembrandt almost fell off!! Replacing his artist's cap sideways on his head, he saw that a bright green moving object was tearing his "masterpiece" apart. Peering closer he shouted, **"Ohh! You bad June bug! You have deeestroyed my best work! Off! Get off my web!!! You must watch where you are flying!!!!!** Now I must start over... Ohh!"

Margaret smiled to Maria, "We had better go on.
Mr. Rembrandt will be worrying over this for hours." Both
girls giggled as they walked on toward the Pond.

The moms were busy setting out picnic goodies and the
dads were tumbling with the youngsters on the grassy hills
by the Pond.

Laurie Duck ran and greeted her friends with hugs and said, "Let's go down to see if there are any new tadpoles!" "OK!!" Margaret was excited, for she loved watching the tadpoles swim around the shallow edges of the pond and change into frogs. Maria said, "No thanks. I don't care for the water very much. We'll all play hop scotch when you come back, OK?" "Great!" they said in unison.

"Margaret," Mother Mouse called out, "remember, you don't know how to swim, so don't get too near the water's edge." "Yes Mom, " Margaret answered absently.

"Skip, skip, skip to my Lou. Skip, skip, skip to my Lou," sang the girls as they skipped happily arm in arm to the water. They sat on a large, flat rock on the bank of the Pond where it poured into Morehouse Creek. They liked this spot because the minnows played in the swirls of water as it rippled over the pebbles.

As girls do, they chattered about school and what they
wanted to be when they grew up. They did not notice the
dark storm clouds gathering.

All of a sudden... **A BRIGHT FLASH!!!** Followed by a **LOUD CRASH OF THUNDER!!** It so startled the girls that Margaret jumped straight up and fell off the rock into the churning stream!!! As the water closed over her head, she bobbed to the surface and screamed, **"Help! I don't know how to swim!!"**

Wrapped in a wet, mushy object that covered her one good eye, Laurie couldn't see. She was of no help to Margaret, quickly swept downstream.

By this time, LARGE drops of rain were spattering upon the water and the wind from the approaching storm had turned the usually calm Pond into a roaring stream! Margaret, terrified, tried to grab anything that floated past her.

Back at the picnic area, the thunder and lightning concerned Mr. Duck. He noticed that Laurie and her friend Margaret had not returned to the shelter. "I'm going to bring the girls back from the Pond," he told the others, waddling slowly on his "feet", actually tiny tennis shoes put on him by his kindly owner when he was born without his normal webbed feet.

As he got near the Pond, Mr. Duck heard screams and saw Laurie splashing in the clutches of what looked like paper. Mr. Duck jumped into the water and paddled his heavy feet toward his daughter. All of a sudden, he felt something brush against him!! He let a sigh of relief to find it was only Cotton, the water snake. **"Help Laurie!"** yelled Mr. Duck, still paddling furiously.

"Don't worry Mr. Duck, I'll get her," Cotton said. Swimming easily over to Laurie, he calmly told her, "Stop struggling. It's only paper that's gotten wet." Managing to free herself, Laurie sputtered, "Margaret! She was swept downstream and she can't swim!!"

"I'll go get her. You go back with your Father," Cotton told her as he swam away.

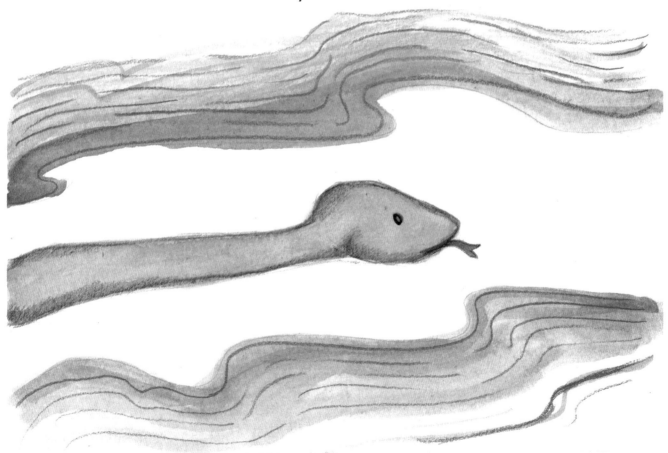

Downstream, Margaret was getting very tired fighting to stay afloat. "Oh! If only I had listened to my parents, I wouldn't be in this mess," she cried.

Further downstream near the Rapids, Samuel Swan was enjoying the rainstorm and Mrs. Swan was teaching Andrew and Jessica about water safety in bad weather. The Swans were a family of black swans who had just moved to Morehouse Creek. They had feathers of shiny black and long, graceful necks with beautiful heads. They were also very big!

SUDDENLY!!!! Samuel stopped and raised his head up high. What was that sound? he thought. Again, he heard what sounded like a feeble *"Help!"* in the distance. He turned to his family, "I'll be back. I must see if someone is in trouble." Because he was big and strong, Samuel could swim against the current. Paddling upstream, something passed by him so quickly he could not tell what it was.

He turned and began paddling to catch up to the object while he thought, That looked very much like a small mouse. As he got closer, he heard a feeble "Help!" coming from the little mouse with tiny arms now splashing up from the water.

Ahead, the sounds of the Rapids could be heard where Morehouse Creek flowed into Riverfront. "I've got to reach that creature before the Rapids," Samuel said out loud beginning to paddle faster.

Margaret knew she was in **BIG TROUBLE!** She caught a glimpse of Willow Tree just ahead, and knew the Rapids were very close. Her tiny head bobbled as she saw a small tree branch sticking out at the water's edge. As she neared the branch she opened her mouth as wide as she could...
CHOMP!!!! Her two big front teeth closed on the branch, which saved her from the Rapids.

Samuel saw the tiny creature stop suddenly near the Rapids. He paddled over and could not believe what he saw! There, attached to a branch by two big front teeth, was a tiny, soggy mouse. He chuckled, "Well, it looks like you are a very lucky little mouse today," as he swam around to get a better look.

"Mumxpth, memxpgh," came the reply.

"Here, grab onto my wing," urged Samuel as he spread his huge wing around Margaret. She grabbed the shiny black feather with the strength she had left. "Now let go of the branch," Samuel encouraged. Margaret let go with her teeth and fell safely into Mr. Swan's wing.

"Hop upon my back," said Mr. Swan as he reached the shore "and I'll take you home." "Who...who...whaa...... what are you?" Margaret asked.

"My name is Samuel and I am a black swan. My family and I moved here to live." "Happy...to...meet...you..." Too exhausted to talk more, Margaret closed her eyes and lay back against Mr. Swan's broad, soft back of feathers, and was instantly asleep.

Back at the picnic area, Margaret's family was very concerned. Cotton had returned without finding her and Mr. Duck had brought Laurie back who told them that Margaret fell into the water. The youngsters were quietly sobbing and Mrs. Mouse worried, "Margaret has never been taught to swim. I pray she is safe."

At that very moment...the bushes parted and a BIG, BLACK creature unlike anything any of them had ever seen approached. Frightened, the duck and mice families backed away. Noticing their fear Samuel said quietly, "There is no need to be afraid of me. I believe I have someone who belongs to you." He then opened his wing to gently lower a still-sleeping Margaret into her Mother's grateful arms.

"**Oh! Thank you!** Thank you, kind sir," both Mouse parents exclaimed in unison. "How can we ever repay you?"

Samuel raised his graceful neck as he thought about the question. Turning to the small group in his quiet voice he said, "Show a kindness to someone in need would be all I could ask of you."

The mouse and duck families watched in wide-eyed wonder as he then turned and walked to the water's edge, swimming gracefully downstream.

***

Moral of this story: Judge not on physical looks, but on character.

"Cherokee Wyatt" spent her early childhood in the mountains of Eastern Tennessee, in true "hillbilly" style, without electricity, indoor plumbing, telephones, or television. "I began writing Margaret's stories as a reflection of my own childhood, which I remember with great fondness. I've created stories that are filled with fun and imaginative characters with differences in race, color, and physical abilities. A moral thought at the end allows children to think about choices and what might happen as a result of those choices.

My wish is that each and every child who reads my books will leave with a   better understanding of themselves and the world around them."

Angela Michelle Redmon is an artist who would like to reintroduce people to the simplicity and purity in thought contained in the child within. A child-like faith that believes the so called "impossible" can and *will* manifest in this lifetime. Once again embracing each moment for its precious, quiet whispers. Causing a renewal out of the learned perspective of reality as taught by the world and becoming hopeful toward the mysteries that await in the excitingly fresh unknown.

In essence — to enjoy life for its unfathomable possibilites and its moments of simple blisses.

Angela is currently developing her own creative line of art products, features and items of practicality known as "Simple Blisses." She seeks God's will in her day to day life and writes as led. She works as a graphic designer in Southern California and is known to frequent the empty stairways in search of enjoying great acoustics while singing.

Dave Woodman works as an animation artist for Disney. His art provided the foundation look for the character, Margaret Mouse, which can be seen on the front cover of this book. Dave also provided some of the early story sketches for this adventure which got the book rolling.